The Elves and the Shoemaker

Anne Walter and Andrew Rowland

W

FRANKLIN WATTS

LONDON • SYDNEY

Chapter 1:
The Shoemaker's Shop

Once upon a time, in a sleepy little town, there lived a shoemaker and his wife. They were very kind, and would often give away the shoes they made to people who couldn't afford to buy them.

Now, giving away shoes is not a good way to make money. So although they worked hard, the shoemaker and his wife were very poor. Before long, the shoemaker had just one piece of leather left.

"There's no more money to buy leather,"
said his wife sadly. "You won't be able to
make any more shoes."

Chapter 2:
The Mystery of the Boots

The poor shoemaker was so unhappy. He left the last piece of leather on the table and went to bed. "I'll have to close the shop for good," he thought.

When the shoemaker woke up the next morning and came downstairs, the leather had disappeared. In its place stood a pair of beautiful, shiny red boots.

The shoemaker couldn't believe his eyes. "Where on earth did these come from?" he wondered. "Who could have made them? What a mystery!"

The shoemaker placed the boots in the shop window. And as soon as the shoemaker opened his shop, a customer came in and bought them.

"These boots are beautiful!" said the customer. "I'll pay you twice what you're asking. Keep making shoes like these and I'll tell all my friends about your shop!"

"Thank you!" said the shoemaker's wife.
"That's enough money to buy leather
for at least two more pairs of shoes.
Don't forget to tell your friends!"

That night, the shoemaker and his wife left the new leather out on the table as before and went to bed.

Chapter 3:
The Mystery of the Shoes

"Do you think we might find some
new boots in the morning?"
whispered the
shoemaker.
"Let's hope
so!" whispered
his wife.

Next morning, they had another surprise.
The leather had gone and in its place stood
two pairs of beautiful, shiny shoes.

The shoemaker placed the new shoes outside his shop. "The stitching is so tiny – it's perfect!" said the shoemaker in amazement. "They certainly are very pretty," his wife agreed, smiling.

The customer from the day before certainly had told his friends about the shoemaker's shop. The two pairs of shoes were sold the instant that the shop opened.

"Now we have enough leather for at least three pairs of shoes!" said the shoemaker's wife happily.

"Business is picking up!" said the shoemaker. "But I just don't understand. I'm the only shoemaker in this town, so who on earth has been making these incredible shoes? We need to thank them for all their help!"

Chapter 4:
The Mystery Helpers

That night, the shoemaker and his wife left the leather on the table as before, but they did not go to bed. They decided to hide behind the curtain and find out who the mystery helpers were. They wanted to say thank you.

17

Before long, the shop window creaked open and two tiny elves hopped through and clambered up onto the shoemaker's table. Giggling and singing merrily, they began cutting the leather into pieces.

The elves seemed happy, but they were dressed in rags and had no shoes on their feet. They didn't know that they were being watched as they folded and stitched the leather.

The shoemaker and his wife looked
on in astonishment.
"I know how we can thank them!"
whispered the shoemaker's wife.
"Let's make them some clothes
      and shoes of their own."

The next evening, as well as the shoe leather, the shoemaker and his wife set out the little clothes and boots they had made. There were two tiny jackets – one in blue and one in red, stripy trousers and smart leather boots.

"I hope they like them," said the shoemaker.

"At least they will be warm!" his wife replied.

As soon as the shop was dark, the little elves
sprang out and hopped onto the table. They
chuckled in delight as they looked at the
little suits and boots, trying them on straight
away. There were even tiny hats to keep their
heads warm.

Chapter 5:
The Elves are Free!

The elves were soon finely dressed – the clothes were a perfect fit! Hopping up and down with excitement, they left the shoe leather on the table and skipped out of the window. Their shoemaking days were over!

When the shoemaker and his wife came down to the shop the next morning, they found some tiny old clothes and the shoe leather, but no new pairs of shoes or boots. The tiny clothes they had made for the elves had disappeared.

"I think they must have liked their new clothes!" laughed the shoemaker's wife.

The shoemaker and his wife never saw their elf helpers again. But they never forgot them. The shop was now famous for its fine shoes and boots and the business thrived.

The shoemaker and his wife never had to worry about money again.

About the story

The Elves and the Shoemaker was included by the Brothers Grimm in their collection of fairytales published in 1812. There are variations of the story, but the shoemaker always appears worthy and willing to help those who are poorer than he is, despite not being rich himself. Elves are a common figure in folklore around the world, and little household helpers appear in many stories. Indeed, the character of Dobby the house elf in the *Harry Potter* stories by J.K. Rowling, is a modern day example of a house elf in literature. Dobby is employed by the Malfoy household, but is freed when Draco Malfoy accidentally gives him a sock.

Be in the story!

Imagine you are the shoemaker and his wife. You are just going to bed and you don't yet know who your helpers are. Who do you think might be making the boots and shoes?

Now imagine you are the elves. What do you want to say to the shoemaker and his wife? Where will you go next?

First published in 2014 by
Franklin Watts
338 Euston Road
London
NW1 3BH

Franklin Watts Australia
Level 17/207 Kent Street
Sydney
NSW 2000

A CIP catalogue record for this book is available
from the British Library.

The artwork for this story first appeared in
Hopscotch Fairytales: The Elves and the Shoemaker

ISBN 978 1 4451 3381 2 (hbk)
ISBN 978 1 4451 3382 9 (pbk)
ISBN 978 1 4451 3383 6 (library ebook)
ISBN 978 1 4451 3384 3 (ebook)

Series Editor: Jackie Hamley
Series Advisor: Catherine Glavina
Series Designer: Cathryn Gilbert

Printed in China

Franklin Watts is a divison of
Hachette Children's Books,
an Hachette UK company.
www.hachette.co.uk